DISNEY FROZEN

SING-ALONG STORYBOOK

"Do You Want to Build a Snowman?" Music and Lyrics by Kristen Anderson-Lopez and Robert Lopez
Published by Wonderland Music Company, Inc. (BMI)

"For the First Time in Forever" Music and Lyrics by Kristen Anderson-Lopez and Robert Lopez
Published by Wonderland Music Company, Inc. (BMI)

"Let It Go" Music and Lyrics by Kristen Anderson-Lopez and Robert Lopez
Published by Wonderland Music Company, Inc. (BMI)
℗2014 Walt Disney Records

For information address Disney Press, 1101 Flower Street, Glendale, California 91201.

Printed in the United States of America

First Edition

1 3 5 7 9 10 8 6 4 2

G942-9090-6-14241

ISBN 978-1-4847-2035-6

For more Disney Press fun, visit www.disneybooks.com

SUSTAINABLE FORESTRY INITIATIVE Certified Sourcing
www.sfiprogram.org
SFI-00993
This Label Applies to Text Stock Only

Disney FROZEN

SING-ALONG Storybook

Adapted by Lisa Marsoli

Illustrated by the Disney Storybook Art Team

Disney PRESS

New York • Los Angeles

THE KINGDOM OF ARENDELLE was a happy place, nestled among the mountains and fjords of the far north. During the day, shopkeepers, fishermen, and ice sellers kept the city bustling. At night, the northern lights lit up the skies in beautiful patterns.

The king and queen of Arendelle had two young daughters,
ELSA and ANNA. The girls were their greatest joy.

But the King and Queen had a secret. Their eldest
daughter, Elsa, had a MAGICAL POWER. She could create
snow and ice with her hands! The King and Queen worried
about what their subjects would think if they knew the
truth. And so Elsa kept the secret from everyone but Anna.

Anna adored her big sister. One night, she convinced
Elsa to turn the Great Hall into a WINTER WONDERLAND.
Elsa filled the room with ice slides. Anna soared
through the air, from slide to slide. "Catch me!" she
shouted, giggling happily.

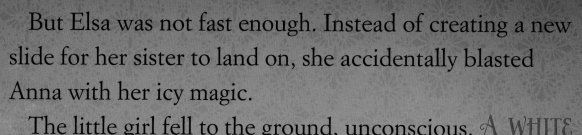

But Elsa was not fast enough. Instead of creating a new slide for her sister to land on, she accidentally blasted Anna with her icy magic.

The little girl fell to the ground, unconscious. A WHITE STREAK APPEARED IN HER HAIR.

Frightened, Elsa called out for help.

The king and queen rushed the girls to the Valley of the Living Rock, where the trolls lived. The trolls were mysterious healers who knew about magic.

"You are lucky it wasn't her heart," a wise old troll named Grand Pabbie said. "The heart is not so easily changed, but the head can be persuaded."

The troll carefully removed all memories of Elsa's magic from Anna's head. "Don't worry," he said. "I'll leave the fun."

Grand Pabbie turned to Elsa. "There is beauty in your magic," he told her, "but also great danger. You must learn to control it. FEAR WILL BE HER ENEMY."

The King and Queen knew they needed to protect their daughter. When they returned to Arendelle, they locked the city gates to keep people away. No one could discover ELSA'S SECRET.

Anna played alone while Elsa worked to control her powers.

But the magic was not so easy to
control. It spilled out any time Elsa felt a
strong emotion. The king gave her gloves
to hold it back, but Elsa was afraid she
might hurt someone by accident. She
even avoided Anna, to keep her little
sister safe.

Anna missed her sister. She often asked Elsa to play, but Elsa always told her to go away.

Then, when the girls were teenagers, the king and queen were lost in a storm at sea. The sisters felt more alone—and apart—than ever.

Elsa stayed inside the castle, where she could hide her magic. But she knew that the day was coming when she would have to open the castle gates. She would become queen when she came of age, and the people of Arendelle must be invited to her coronation.

Finally, the day arrived. People streamed into Arendelle.

Anna was thrilled at the chance to meet new people—and maybe even FALL IN LOVE.

But Elsa was worried about being the center of attention. What if her powers accidentally came out?

Anna slipped outside and strolled around the
kingdom. A handsome visitor—Prince Hans of
the Southern Isles—accidentally bumped into
her on his horse. Hans and Anna were instantly
smitten with each other.

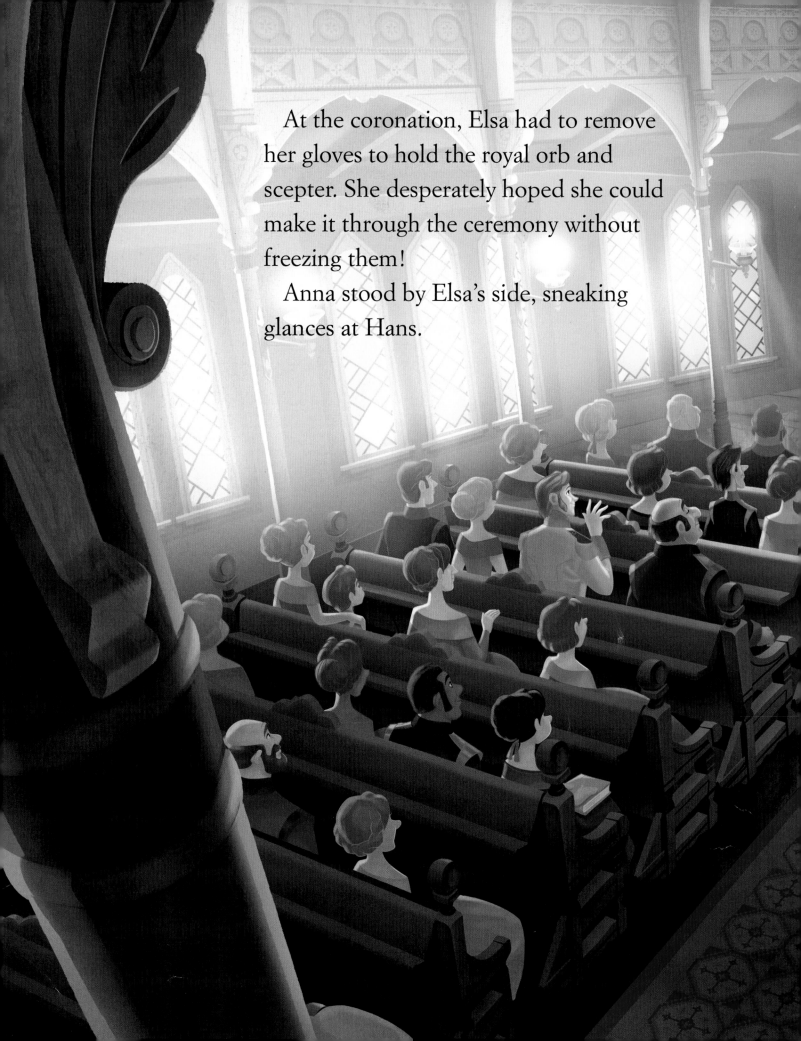

At the coronation, Elsa had to remove her gloves to hold the royal orb and scepter. She desperately hoped she could make it through the ceremony without freezing them!

Anna stood by Elsa's side, sneaking glances at Hans.

At the Coronation Ball, Hans and Anna spent the whole evening laughing, dancing, and talking.

IT WAS LOVE AT FIRST SIGHT...

so they got engaged!

Elsa was shocked. "You can't marry a man you just met," she scoffed.

"YOU CAN IF IT'S TRUE LOVE," Anna insisted.

"My answer is no," Elsa said firmly, refusing to allow the marriage.

Elsa started to leave the room, but Anna grabbed her hand—AND ACCIDENTALLY PULLED OFF HER GLOVE.

Anna kept arguing. "Why do you shut me out?"
she asked Elsa. "I can't live like this anymore!"
"ENOUGH!" Elsa cried.

A freezing blast shot from Elsa's bare hand, sending a sheet of ice across the ballroom! Everyone stared in disbelief.

Elsa fled the castle, terrified that she might hurt someone. "STAY AWAY FROM ME," she warned the townspeople.

Everything Elsa touched turned to ice as she
ran. Even the fjord froze as she stepped onto the
water. All the ships became trapped in the ice.

The people of Arendelle panicked as the ice spread through the kingdom. ANNA KNEW SHE HAD TO DO SOMETHING. Leaving Hans in charge, she set out to find Elsa and bring her back to thaw out the kingdom.

Meanwhile, Elsa climbed high into the mountains. With no one else to worry about, SHE LET HER POWERS LOOSE. A storm raged around her as she created ice sculptures, made a snowman, and even transformed the way she looked.

As she neared the top of the
mountain, ELSA CREATED A
MAGNIFICENT, SHINING ICE PALACE.
She felt like the person she was
always meant to be! She was alone,
but she also was, at long last,
entirely herself.

Anna, meanwhile, couldn't wait to reunite with her sister. Now that Elsa's secret was out, they could finally be close again!

The storm made the journey difficult, though— especially when Anna's horse threw her into the snow. Luckily, she spotted a small building up ahead.

Inside Wandering Oaken's Trading Post and Sauna, Anna gathered up boots and some warm clothes.

Then a young man named Kristoff trudged in.
He was an ice harvester and very unhappy that the
surprise summer storm was ruining his business!

When Kristoff mentioned that the storm was coming from the North Mountain, Anna pestered him with questions. She wanted information about Elsa.

But Kristoff was busy bargaining with Oaken. "Back up while I deal with this crook!" he told Anna.

An insulted Oaken THREW KRISTOFF OUT!

That gave Anna an idea. She found Kristoff in
the stable with his reindeer, Sven, and gave him the
supplies he needed. In return, she asked that he take
her up the North Mountain.

Finally, Kristoff agreed. "We leave at dawn."

"We leave now," Anna said. "RIGHT NOW."

On the way, Anna told Kristoff what had happened in Arendelle. It all sounded strange to Kristoff, but he hoped Anna could convince Elsa to bring back summer so that people would need his ice again. Suddenly, they heard wolves howling.

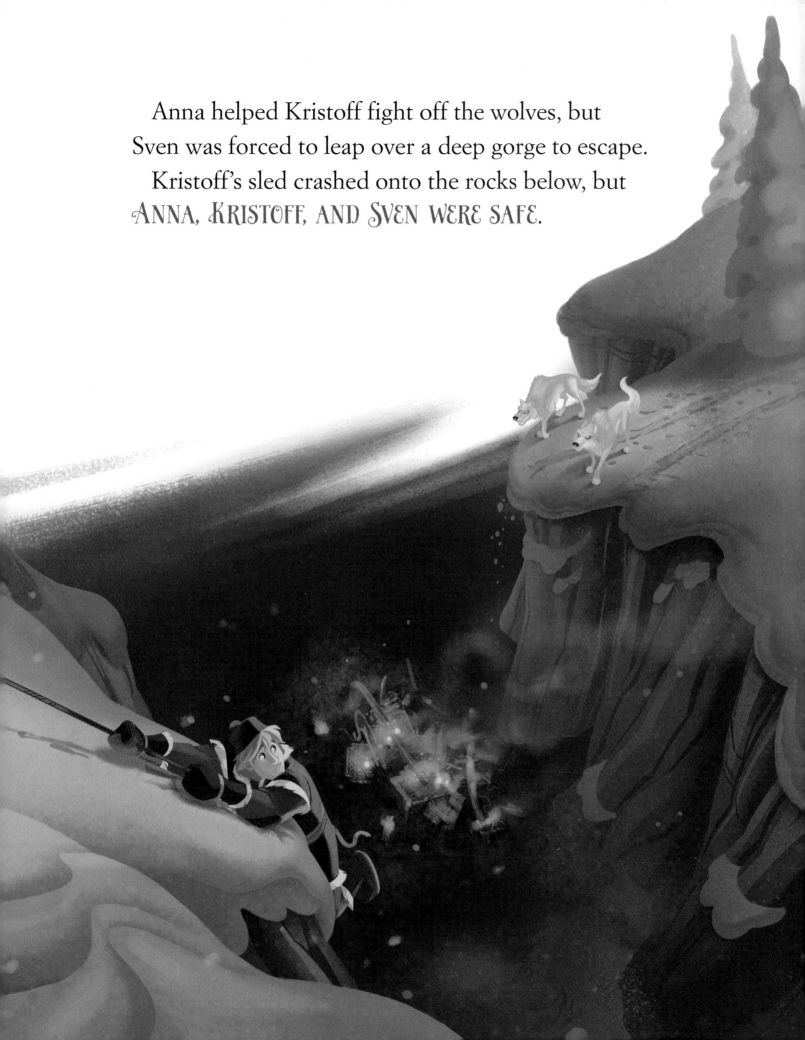

Anna helped Kristoff fight off the wolves, but
Sven was forced to leap over a deep gorge to escape.
Kristoff's sled crashed onto the rocks below, but
ANNA, KRISTOFF, AND SVEN WERE SAFE.

As dawn broke, Anna and Kristoff could see
Arendelle far below at the bottom of the mountain.
To their dismay, the kingdom was still locked in winter.
Then they hiked farther into the forest, where Elsa's
icy powers had created a spectacular scene.

"I NEVER KNEW WINTER COULD BE SO . . .
BEAUTIFUL," Anna said in wonder.

"But it's so white," added a voice. "How about a
little color? I'm thinking like maybe some crimson,
chartreuse . . ."

Behind them was a living snowman! "I'm Olaf,"
he said and explained that Elsa had made him.
Anna asked Olaf to lead them to her sister. "We
need Elsa to bring back summer."

"I've always loved the idea of summer," said Olaf, smiling. "My snow up against the burning sand . . . getting gorgeously tanned. . . ."

But Anna and Kristoff both had the same thought: summer would *not* be good for a snowman.

Back in Arendelle, Hans was trying to keep everyone calm. One of the visiting dignitaries, a duke, was especially angry about being stuck in the frozen kingdom.

Then Anna's horse showed up without her.

"PRINCESS ANNA IS IN TROUBLE," Hans called out. "I need volunteers to go with me to find her!"

The Duke insisted that his men join the search party.

Meanwhile, the path up the mountain was getting very steep. Luckily, Olaf found a stairway made of ice leading straight to Elsa's palace.

"Whoa," said Anna in awe as they reached the top. THE PALACE WAS AMAZING!

Elsa wasn't happy to see Anna. She was
afraid of hurting Anna with her icy powers.
"YOU SHOULD PROBABLY GO," Elsa
warned Anna.

But Anna explained that Arendelle needed Elsa's help. The kingdom was freezing, and no one knew what to do.

Now Elsa was frightened. She admitted that she couldn't unfreeze the kingdom. SHE DIDN'T KNOW HOW!

Anna was sure they could figure it out together, but Elsa just grew more upset. Frustrated, Elsa cried out, "I CAN'T!"

An icy blast shot across the room and hit Anna in the chest!

Kristoff rushed to help Anna. "I think we should go," he said.

"No! I'm not leaving without you!" Anna told her sister.

"YES, YOU ARE," Elsa replied, conjuring up a giant snowman.

Elsa ordered the huge snowman to escort Anna and her companions off the mountain. But after Anna hit him with a snowball, he decided to chase them instead!

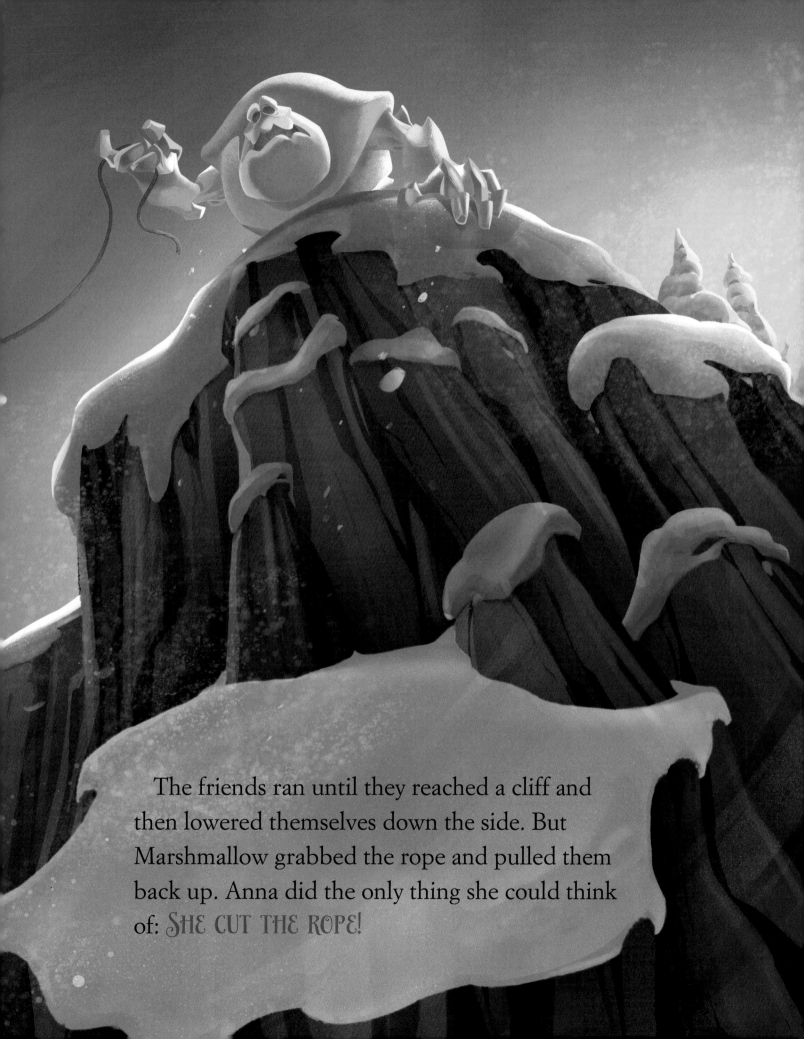

The friends ran until they reached a cliff and then lowered themselves down the side. But Marshmallow grabbed the rope and pulled them back up. Anna did the only thing she could think of: SHE CUT THE ROPE!

Luckily, Anna, Kristoff, and Olaf landed safely in a soft snowdrift down below. But something was wrong with Anna: HER HAIR WAS TURNING WHITE.

"It's because she struck you, isn't it?" Kristoff asked.

Concerned about Anna, Kristoff came up with a plan.

"You need help," he said. "Now, come on."
"Where are we going?" Olaf asked.
"To see my friends," Kristoff answered.

Back at the ice palace, Elsa paced back and
forth, trying to figure out how she could unfreeze
Arendelle. ELSA WAS VERY UPSET, which made
her powers more difficult to control. And that
made the storm grow even worse.

Night fell as Kristoff led Anna, Olaf, and Sven into a remote and rocky valley. Kristoff said that his friends lived there.

Suddenly, Anna thought she saw some
of the rocks move.
"TROLLS!" she exclaimed.

Kristoff had spent a lot of time with the trolls.
In fact, he was practically family to them. He
knew they could help Anna.

The trolls were very excited to meet Anna. They thought she was Kristoff's girlfriend! The trolls thought it was a great match—love brings out the best in everyone!

But Grand Pabbie realized that Anna was hurt. "Anna, your life is in danger," he said. "There is ice in your heart, put there by your sister. If not removed, to solid ice you will freeze, forever." Grand Pabbie explained that only an act of true love could thaw a frozen heart.

Olaf and Kristoff decided to take Anna back home. Surely Prince Hans could break the spell with a true love's kiss.

At that same moment, Hans and the search party were arriving at Elsa's ice palace. MARSHMALLOW TRIED TO PROTECT THE QUEEN, but the mob attacked him.

The men burst into the palace.
The Duke's men attacked Elsa.

As her worry and fear grew,
so did her powers. She created
a huge wall of ice that pushed
one of the Duke's men to the
edge of the balcony. Icy spikes
quickly pinned the other man
against a wall.

Just then, Hans called out, "DON'T BE THE MONSTER THEY FEAR YOU ARE!"

Elsa realized she had let her magic go too far. She let her hands drop. The men were safe.

Suddenly, one of the men aimed a crossbow at Elsa! Hans pushed it aside so the arrow hit the chandelier. It crashed to the ground, knocking Elsa out.

Elsa woke up in a cell in the castle. Gazing out the window, she was shocked to see how her storm had damaged the kingdom.

When she asked for Anna, Hans said her sister hadn't returned.

Outside, Anna, Kristoff, and Olaf were hurrying down the mountain. KRISTOFF WAS WORRIED. It was clear that Anna was getting weaker.

At the castle gates, he passed her to the royal servants. He was starting to realize that he cared deeply about Anna but knew that her true love, Hans, could make her well again.

The servants rushed Anna to the library where Hans had been meeting with the dignitaries. Shivering, Anna explained what Elsa's icy blast had done and how his kiss could cure her. "ONLY AN ACT OF TRUE LOVE CAN SAVE ME," she said.

"Oh, Anna," Hans sneered. "IF ONLY THERE WAS SOMEONE OUT THERE WHO LOVED YOU."

As he doused the fire, Hans explained that he had pretended to love Anna in order to take over Arendelle. All that was left, he told her, was to get rid of Elsa. "I am the hero who is going to save Arendelle from destruction," he said.

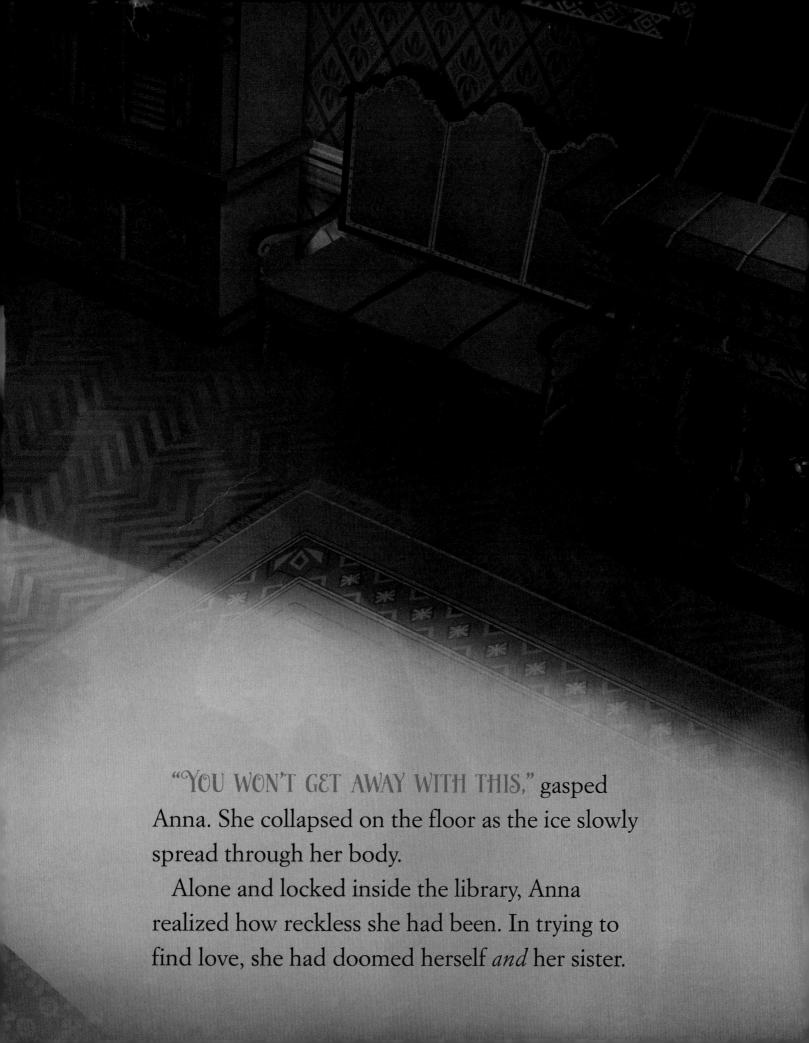

"YOU WON'T GET AWAY WITH THIS," gasped Anna. She collapsed on the floor as the ice slowly spread through her body.

Alone and locked inside the library, Anna realized how reckless she had been. In trying to find love, she had doomed herself *and* her sister.

Hans returned to the dignitaries and told them that Elsa had killed Anna! HE CONTINUED LYING, describing how he and Anna had exchanged marriage vows before she died.

"I charge Queen Elsa of Arendelle with treason and sentence her to death," he declared.

In the dungeon, all Elsa could think about was getting away from Arendelle. It was the only way to protect everyone from her powers. Elsa became so upset that she froze the whole dungeon and escaped!

Meanwhile, Kristoff was heading up the mountain, but Sven forced him to stop. THE REINDEER THOUGHT THAT KRISTOFF WAS ANNA'S REAL TRUE LOVE.

Then Kristoff saw a violent storm over Arendelle. He ran back toward the kingdom. He had to help Anna!

Just when Anna had given up all hope, Olaf arrived. The snowman lit a fire, even though Anna worried that he might melt. "SOME PEOPLE ARE WORTH MELTING FOR," he said.

Then Olaf looked out the window and saw Kristoff returning. The snowman realized that Kristoff was the true love who could save Anna!

Olaf helped Anna outside, where she spotted
Kristoff across the frozen fjord. If she could reach
Kristoff in time, she would be saved!

But then she saw something else: HANS WAS
ABOUT TO STRIKE ELSA WITH HIS SWORD!

With her remaining strength, Anna threw herself
in front of Elsa. Hans's sword came down just as
ANNA'S BODY FROZE TO SOLID ICE.

With a loud *CLANK*, the blade shattered.

Elsa wrapped her arms around her frozen sister. "Oh, Anna," she sobbed.

Then something amazing happened: Anna began to thaw! "You sacrificed yourself for me?" Elsa asked.

"I love you," replied Anna weakly.

"AN ACT OF TRUE LOVE WILL THAW A FROZEN HEART," Olaf said, realizing what had happened.

That's when Elsa realized that love could bring back summer. She raised her arms and the snow melted away. The people of Arendelle cheered. They had seen everything that had happened.

BUT OLAF WAS MELTING, TOO! Elsa quickly made him his own little snow cloud to keep him safe.

Hans was astonished to see Anna alive. "Anna?" he
said. "But she froze your heart."

"THE ONLY FROZEN HEART AROUND HERE IS YOURS!"
Anna said and sent him reeling with one punch.

With summer restored, the visiting ships sailed away, and Arendelle returned to normal—but now the castle gates were open for good!

Anna replaced Kristoff's sled and his supplies. But he wasn't anxious to leave—ESPECIALLY WHEN ANNA SURPRISED HIM WITH A KISS.

Elsa created an ice-skating rink and welcomed everyone in the kingdom. The people of Arendelle had a wonderful time skating with Queen Elsa and Princess Anna.

At long last, THE KINGDOM OF ARENDELLE WAS A HAPPY PLACE ONCE MORE.

Do you know
every word to "LET IT GO"?
How about "DO YOU WANT TO
BUILD A SNOWMAN?" or "FOR THE
FIRST TIME IN FOREVER"? Well now
you can carry the lyrics with you!

Just turn the page to see the words to
your favorite *Frozen* songs. Then put
in your CD to sing along. You'll
be singing like Anna and
Elsa in no time!

Do You Want to Build a Snowman?

Music and Lyrics by Kristen Anderson-Lopez and Robert Lopez
Published by Wonderland Music Company, Inc. (BMI)

Young Anna:

Elsa?
Do you want to build a snowman?
Come on, let's go and play!
I never see you anymore
Come out the door
It's like you've gone away

We used to be best buddies
And now we're not
I wish you would tell me why!

Do you want to build a snowman?
It doesn't have to be a snowman . . .

Young Elsa:

Go away, Anna.

Young Anna:

Okay, bye . . .

Teen Anna:

Do you want to build a snowman?
Or ride our bike around the halls?
I think some company is overdue
I've started talking to
The pictures on the walls!

Hang in there, Joan.

It gets a little lonely
All these empty rooms
Just watching the hours tick by . . .
Tic-Tock, Tic-Tock, Tic-Tock, Tic-Tock, Tic-Tock

Anna:

Elsa?
Please, I know you're in there
People are asking where you've been
They say "have courage," and I'm trying to
I'm right out here for you
Just let me in

We only have each other
It's just you and me
What are we gonna do?

Do you want to build a snowman?

For the First Time in Forever

Music and Lyrics by Kristen Anderson-Lopez and Robert Lopez
Published by Wonderland Music Company, Inc. (BMI)

Anna:

The window is open!
So's that door!
I didn't know they did that anymore!
Who knew we owned eight thousand salad plates . . . ?

For years I've roamed these empty halls
Why have a ballroom with no balls?
Finally they're opening up the gates!

There'll be actual real live people
It'll be totally strange
But wow! Am I so ready for this change!

'Cause for the first time in forever
There'll be music, there'll be light!
For the first time in forever
I'll be dancing through the night . . .
Don't know if I'm elated or gassy
But I'm somewhere in that zone!
'Cause for the first time in forever
I won't be alone

I can't wait to meet everyone!
What if I meet THE ONE?

Tonight, imagine me gown and all
Fetchingly draped against the wall
The picture of sophisticated grace . . .

I suddenly see him standing there
A beautiful stranger, tall and fair
I wanna stuff some chocolate in my face!

But then we laugh and talk all evening
Which is totally bizarre
Nothing like the life I've led so far!

For the first time in forever
There'll be magic, there'll be fun!
For the first time in forever
I could be noticed by someone . . .
And I know it is totally crazy
To dream I'd find romance . . .
But for the first time in forever
At least I've got a chance!

Elsa:

Don't let them in
Don't let them see
Be the good girl
You always have to be
Conceal
Don't feel
Put on a show . . .
Make one wrong move
And everyone will know

But it's only for today

Anna:

It's only for today!

Elsa:

It's agony to wait

Anna:

It's agony to wait

Elsa:

Tell the guards to open up the gate!

Anna:

The gate!!!
For the first time in forever

Elsa:

Don't let them in, don't let them see

Anna:

I'm getting what I'm dreaming of!

Elsa:

Be the good girl you always have to be

Anna:

A chance to change my lonely world

Elsa:

Conceal

Anna:

A chance to find true love!

Elsa:

Conceal, don't feel
Don't let them know

Anna:

I know it all ends tomorrow
So it has to be today!
'Cause for the first time in forever . . .
For the first time in forever
Nothing's in my way!!!

Let It Go

Music and Lyrics by Kristen Anderson-Lopez and Robert Lopez
Published by Wonderland Music Company, Inc. (BMI)

The snow glows white
On the mountain tonight
Not a footprint to be seen
A kingdom of isolation
And it looks like I'm the Queen

The wind is howling
Like this swirling storm inside
Couldn't keep it in
Heaven knows I've tried . . .

Don't let them in
Don't let them see
Be the good girl you always had to be
Conceal, don't feel
Don't let them know . . .
Well, now they know!

Let it go, let it go
Can't hold it back anymore
Let it go, let it go
Turn away and slam the door!
I don't care what they're going to say
Let the storm rage on
The cold never bothered me anyway

It's funny how some distance
Makes everything seems small
And the fears that once controlled me
Can't get to me at all!

It's time to see
What I can do
To test the limits and break through
No right, no wrong
No rules for me
I'm free!

Let it go! Let it go!
I am one with the wind and sky!
Let it go! Let it go!
You'll never see me cry!
Here I stand and here I'll stay
Let the storm rage on. . . .

My power flurries through the air into the ground
My soul is spiraling in frozen fractals all around
And one thought crystallizes like an icy blast
I'm never going back
The past is in the past!

Let it go! Let it go!
And I'll rise like the break of dawn!
Let it go! Let it go!
That perfect girl is gone!

Here I stand in the light of day . . .
Let the storm rage on!!!
The cold never bothered me anyway!